SAM

&

DAVE

DIG

A

HOLE

Mac Barnett

illustrated by

Jon Klassen

WALKER BOOKS
AND SUBSIDIARIES
LONDON · BOSTON · SYDNEY · AUCKLAND

On Monday Sam and Dave dug a hole.

"When should we stop digging?" asked Sam.

"We are on a mission," said Dave.

"We won't stop digging until we find
   something spectacular."

The hole got so deep that their heads
were underground.
But they still had not found anything
spectacular.
"We need to keep digging," said Dave.

So they kept digging.

They took a break.

Dave drank chocolate milk

out of a flask.

Sam ate animal biscuits he had wrapped

in their grandfather's kerchief.

"Maybe," said Dave,

"the problem is that we are

digging straight down."

"Yes," said Sam.

"That could be the problem."

"I think we should dig in

another direction," said Dave.

"Yes," said Sam.

"That is a good idea."

"I have a new idea," said Dave.

"Let's split up."

"Really?" said Sam.

"Just for a little while," said Dave.

"It will improve our chances."

So Dave went one way,

and Sam went another.

But they did not find anything spectacular.

"Maybe we should go back to digging straight down," said Dave.

"Yes," said Sam.

"That is a good idea."

Sam and Dave ran out of chocolate milk.

But they kept digging.

They shared the last animal biscuit.

But they kept digging.

After a while Sam sat down.

"Dave," he said, "I am tired.

I cannot dig any more."

"I am tired too," said Dave.

"We should have a rest."

Sam and Dave fell asleep.

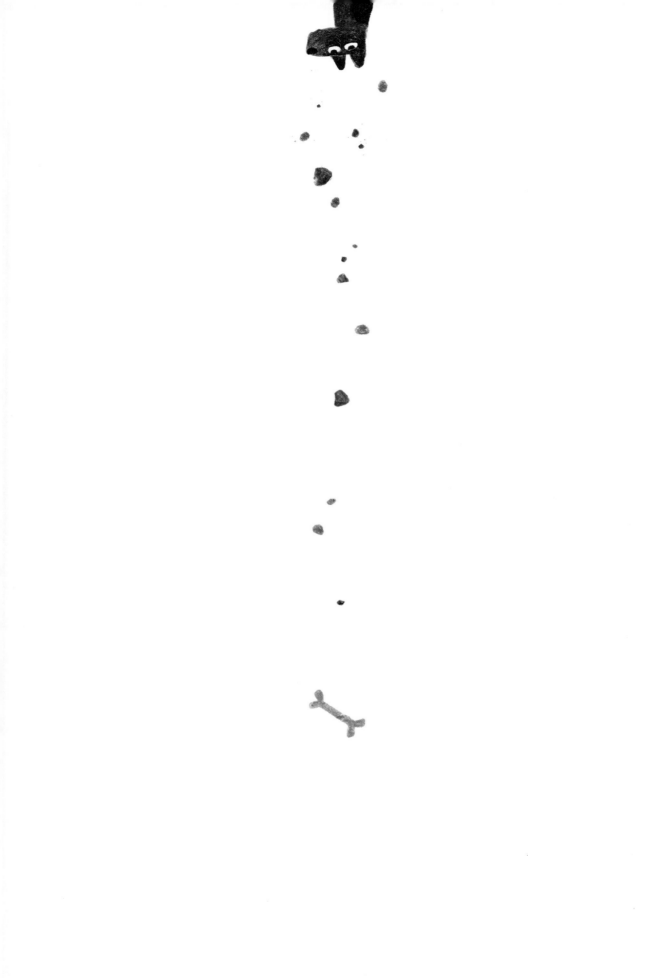

Then Sam and Dave were falling.

Sam and Dave fell down,

down,

down,

until they landed in the soft earth.

"Well," said Sam.

"Well," said Dave.

"That was pretty spectacular."

And they went inside

for chocolate milk and animal biscuits.

For Carson Ellis
M. B.

For St Davids, Ontario
J. K.

First published 2014 by Walker Books Ltd
87 Vauxhall Walk, London SE11 5HJ

4 6 8 10 9 7 5

Text © 2014 Mac Barnett
Illustrations © 2014 Jon Klassen

The right of Mac Barnett and Jon Klassen to be identified as author and illustrator respectively of this work
has been asserted by them in accordance with the Copyright, Designs and Patents Act 1988

This book has been typeset in Minion Pro

Printed in China

British Library Cataloguing in Publication Data:
a catalogue record for this book is available from the British Library

ISBN 978-1-4063-5776-9

www.walker.co.uk